Okay, so I just want to mention a few things before you start reading the next part of my diary (or journal or memoirs or WHATEVER).

First of all, I usually like to start each new entry with a date . . . but in Abadazad (if you don't know what Abadazad is . . . and maybe a few of you don't . . . it's this place that I USED to think only existed in books . . . till this old lady who lived across the hall gave me a magical blue globe that sent me there. And, no, I'm not kidding) time gets so weird and fuzzy, and their calendar is so confusing, that I couldn't keep track . . . which is why I pretty much dropped the date thing and just wrote NEW ENTRY for each section.

Another thing: you're gonna read this and wonder how I can remember EVERY word of EVERY conversation so perfectly. Answer: I CAN'T. I mean, I've got a pretty good memory, but mostly for useless stuff like what year Thrashing Plague first played Madison Square Garden or what's on every cable channel at just about any time of the day or night (Frances calls me "The Walking TV Guide." It's not a compliment). Best I can figure is that the diary . . . which, ridiculous as it sounds, is ENCHANTED . . . kind of helped me to remember things I normally couldn't.

Then there's my spelling . . . which is one of the few school-type things I'm good at. I never study but I pretty much ace the tests every week. As good as I am, though, I still make my share of mistakes . . . but every time I mangled some poor word in the diary, THE WORD CORRECTED ITSELF. RIGHT IN FRONT OF ME. (Hey, maybe I could sell this to Apple or Microsoft: the world's first magical spell-checker.)

So anyway . . . here's what happened to me that first night in the Floating City of Inconceivable. I was TOTALLY WIRED because Queen Ija promised that she'd help me rescue my brother Matty . . . who'd been missing for five years . . . from the Lanky Man (if you're new to the story, just take my word for all this: it's WAY too complicated to explain), but I finally managed to fall asleep and . . . Well, just read it, okay? This stuff's even weirder than the stuff in the last book . . . but every word of it is true. I SWEAR.

The average idiot on the street would think I'm making this up, but I figure if you're reading this you're NOT an average idiot. You're probably the kind of person who BELIEVES that there's more to this stupid world than the garbage they shove down our throats every night on the six o'clock news. And . . . as Queen Ija once told me . . . when it comes to magic, believing's the MOST IMPORTANT THING.

Kate

Headstrong, his sodden hair hanging in his face. "With the soaking you've given me, it will take hours to restore my curls to their natural state of buoyancy."

"Vanity, vanity," interjected Mary, but Headstrong ignored her, as he often did.

"My sincere apologies, Professor," wheezed Mr. Gloom, "but it seems . . ." He paused to let fly another thunderous sneeze that nearly knocked Mary Annette off her feet and sent Headstrong scurrying for cover. "It seems," he continued, snuffling, "that these Peppernuts are irritating my ever-so sensitive nose."

"Irritating?" exclaimed Princess Popperpep. Her little face reddened, and anger flashed through those bright green eyes. "Why, we have never been so insulted in all our years!"

"Might I remind the Princess," whispered High Lord Cashoo, whose desire for accuracy outweighed his natural timidity, "that you were only plucked from the Royaltree this morning. You have not yet lived a single day, let alone a year."

"And might we remind His Lordship," the Princess snarled, rounding on her counselor with such ferocity that

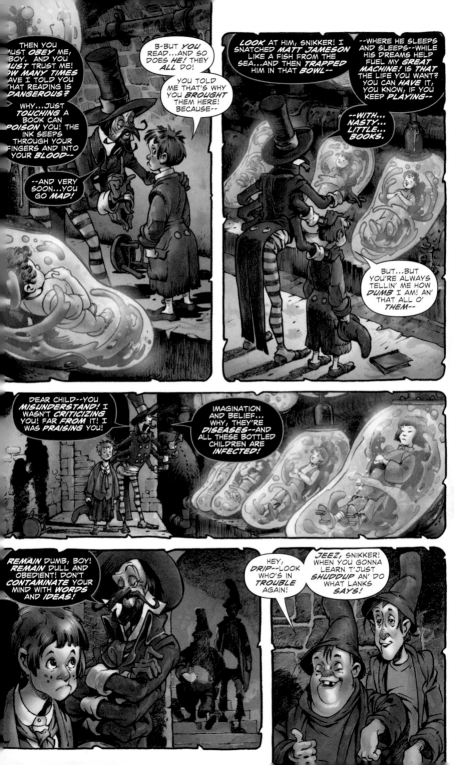

"What NOW?" I groaned. Y'see, I sleep on this ancient foldout couch in the living room (the mattress is so thin I've got spring marks all over my back and I'm NOT exaggerating. Much) and, lucky me, the living-room windows face the front of the building. Which means that all night long I hear fire engines screaming, ambulances wailing, cop cars blasting their sirens. And let's not forget the city buses bouncing down Seventh Avenue and rattling the whole house and, best of all, the assorted late-night lunatics who like to hang out on our front steps, howling like drunken coyotes.

Most of the time I can sleep through it . . . I mean, you live in the Big City your whole life and you get used to this stuff (either that or you ABANDON YOUR FAMILY and move to Seattle or Portland, or wherever it is Herbert the Great ran off to). But every once in a while it gets SO noisy that I have to drag myself out of bed and see what the heck is going on. (Frantic Frances, on the other hand, can sleep through anything. If a brontosaurus came lumbering through the apartment, she'd just throw another pillow over her head and keep snoring.)

So I jump out of bed (okay, I FALL out)

and look around, and all of a sudden I'm confused. Where's the ten-year-old TV, the broken VCR (I must be the only kid in the ninth grade without a DVD player), and the ratty old furniture? I climb back onto the couch—only I realize it's NOT the couch, it's a bed . . . a humongoid bed, with a mattress so soft that it feels like it's made out of clouds. (I found out later that it actually was.) So now I'm really confused. Then I look up and see the painting of the Floating Warlock on the wall—and I remember: I'm not in Brooklyn. I don't even know if I'm on Earth.

I'm in ABADAZAD.

All of it comes back to me: Mrs. Vaughn and the Blue Globe. The Shelloppers and Sour Flowers. The Living Staircase. Little Martha. Queen Ija.

MATT!

I was in the Floating City of Inconceivable . . . my brother was alive . . . and Queen Ija herself was gonna help me rescue him.

I started jumping around the room—pumping my fist in the air, shouting "Yes! Yes! Yes!"—and then the world started wobbling again . . . the entire palace rocking back and forth like we were inside one of those shake-'em-up Christmas snow globes. A lamp toppled off the night table (although it stopped like a quarter of an inch before it hit the floor and sailed back up again. Guess it helps to have enchanted furniture), and I fell flat on my butt. I don't have a lot of padding down there and it really hurt.

I scrambled to my feet and ran to the balcony, sure that there must have been some kind of earthquake. (Okay, so you can't HAVE an earthquake if you're in a city in the sky. So maybe it was a cloud-quake or something. What do you want from me? I was half asleep). But it wasn't an earthquake. It was worse than that: It was the ROCKET HEADS.

For the two of you out there who've never read Franklin O. Davies's Abadazad books and have no clue what a Rocket Head is, let me get you up to speed: they were these bizzaro creatures—created by the Lanky Man—that could shoot off their heads like (duh) rockets and then EXPLODE them into thousands of pieces. (This didn't kill them—no one ever died in an Abadazad book, not even the bad guys—they'd just grow NEW heads and start blasting them off again.)

Every few books, Lanks would send the R-Heads out to invade the capital city. And every few books they'd fail. Miserably. But as weird as they were with their swollen skulls and gigantic bat-ears, they always seemed more silly than threatening. In fact, when they made the Abadazad cartoon show, the Rockets were the funniest thing on it. Saint Matt used to roll around on the living-room floor, laughing HIS head off whenever they shot off THEIRS. (The heads never actually exploded in the cartoons. Guess the Network Censors were afraid they'd traumatize the kiddies.)

But those REAL Rocket Heads were a whole different story. I mean, seeing some goofy animated characters blasting their heads off on TV is one thing. Seeing it in real life is another. (If I can even CALL this "real life." But I guess it is. In a totally UNreal way.) And there were dozens of them . . . flying around in these balloon gizmos . . . zooming toward the palace . . . launching their heads at us like guided missiles. Smashing right through the walls.

Considering my brother'd been kidnapped by the Lanky Man, it didn't take a genius to figure out that Lanks had sent the Rockets after me. But what I didn't get was why he waited till I came to Inconceivable. I mean, if he could grab Matty back in our world, how come he didn't take me then, too?

I didn't have much time to think about that because right then two Rocket Heads came crashing through the wall of my bedroom. They were Super-Balling around, bouncing off the walls and laughing (not HA-HA laughing, more like the laughing mad scientists do in old black-and-white movies) trying to get their slimy hands on me. Okay, so they didn't HAVE hands. But they didn't need them: once they got close enough to do their human bomb routine, I'd be blown out of Abadazad and halfway across New Jersey. (And if you've ever been to New Jersey, you know that's not exactly a place you want to end up.)

I sprinted out of the room and down the hall, going faster than I EVER ran in gym class (well, the truth is I almost never ran in gym class because I almost never WENT to gym class. I mean what's the point of getting all smelly and sweaty and then, worse! having to take a shower with a bunch of other smelly,

sweaty girls?), but those R-Heads were behind me—BOINK! BOINK! BOINK!—getting closer every second.

Little Martha (funny how that dumb name starts to grow on you after a while) was staying just down the hall—we were sharing our own private wing—so I started running for her apartment and screaming her name . . . only I was so winded, all that came out was this pathetic little wheeze. (Okay, so maybe I should have gone to gym a couple of times.) Figured my best bet was to grab Martha and head for the Throne Room, 'cause if anyone could stop the attack it was Queen Ija.

Now don't think stopping to get Martha makes me brave or anything. Sure, I was worried about her—but the sad truth is I had NO CLUE how to get to the Throne Room without Martha's help. I don't exactly have a finely tuned sense of direction. My mother says I can get lost going from the living room to the bathroom. Which is a really mean thing to say. True . . . but mean.

So I'm racing down the corridor and those Rocket Heads are so close now I'm sucking down their exhaust—car exhaust smells like PERFUME by comparison—and I finally make it to

Martha's place, hustle myself in there and slam the door . . . just waiting for the two Rockets to come crashing through after me.

But they didn't..

They just hung around in the hall, bouncing up and down, up and down . . . and if my nerves weren't shot ALREADY, listening to that sound over and over—BOINK, boink, BOINK, boink, BOINK, boink—pretty much did it. I knew they could get in any time they wanted, but aside from maybe fainting or peeing all over myself—neither of which seemed like very good options—I couldn't think of what to do.

I called out for Martha—she was used to this crazy stuff, and I figured (well, hoped) she'd have some kind of Rocket Head Emergency Plan all worked out—but she wasn't there. I started to get REALLY worried then. What if she was in trouble? What if the Heads had hurt her or . . . worse . . . taken her prisoner? What if they were dragging her off to the Wretchedly Awful City, to be locked away with Matty and the rest of those poor kids the Lanky Man had kidnapped?

I was slipping into a state of hysteria that

would've made Frantic Frances proud when—BOINK, BOINK, BOINK, BOINK—I heard the Rocket Heads bouncing down the hall AWAY FROM ME. And then . . . dead quiet.

It's a trick, I thought. It's gotta be a trick. Whatever you do, don't open the door!

But, really, what choice did I have? I opened the door . . . just the tiniest bit . . . and peeked out.

Nobody there.

Feeling a little braver (or maybe just a little less scared), I inched out into the corridor. All clear.

Maybe, I thought, the Endless Knight or the Burning Witch had arrived and butt-kicked the R-Heads all the way back to the Wretchedly Awful City. Or maybe Ija had called out the Abadazadian army, and those Rockets were more scared now than I was and sonic-booming home to their scuzzball master with their tails between their legs (okay, okay, so they don't have tails OR legs . . . but you know what I mean). Maybe—

And then the door across the hall creaked open.

And two sneering Rocket Heads zoomed out—straight at me.

And

everything

just

BLEW

UP

!!!

Next thing I knew, I was tumbling through the air at a gazillion miles an hour . . . my ears were ringing like Christmas bells . . . my stomach was on a joyride into my throat . . . and I couldn't tell if I was moving up, down, or sideways. (Actually, it felt like all three directions at once.)

Right up ahead of me was this humongoid door, which, at the speed I was going, would pretty much turn me into one of those mosquito splotches you find on your windshield in the summer.

Now, in the books, the Rocket Heads never actually HURT anybody. Sure, people would get blasted into the stratosphere, but they always managed to land in a convenient tree branch or some cushy field. But that was fiction—and I'd already seen that the real Abadazad and the one in Davies's stories didn't exactly match up.

So here comes that door, right? And I start thinking about what a rotten person I've been for most of my life (and don't be so quick to agree!), and how if, by some miracle, I'm spared being turned into a splotch, I'll try really REALLY hard to at least be a little nicer.

But just as I'm about to slam, headfirst, right into it . . . the door swings open—and then THUNDERS shut right behind me!

I hit the ground hard and started boinking along on my butt (which, as I've already mentioned, isn't exactly well padded) like I was a Rocket Head . . . flopping forward and landing flat on my fat face.

Then someone walked up to me.

From my cockroach-level perspective, all I could see were ankles and shoes (ugly shoes, too. Dirt brown with these horrendous gold buckles). My first thought was, Hey, those flying heads don't HAVE ankles and they don't WEAR shoes, so Mr. or Ms. Ugly Footwear must be one of the Good Guys, right? But then I started to wonder if maybe the Lanky Man had come to Inconceivable along WITH his nasty little homeboys, and maybe THIS WAS HIM . . . ready to stuff me in his Dwindlebox (like he did to Little Martha in Book Fourteen, *The Two-Fold Witch of Abadazad*. Remember? She was half an inch tall for almost a hundred pages), shove me in his back pocket, and take me away.

Then Whoever It Was said "Hiya," and I relaxed a little—'cause I could tell from the voice that it was just a kid. A boy kid, from the sound of it. The room was pretty dark—just a little moonlight washing in through the stained-glass windows—but, from the little I could see, he seemed about Matty's size.

"Uh . . . hi," I said, struggling to my feet. "Was that you who opened the door?"

"NUH-uh," the kid answered. "The doors did it themselves."

"Right," I said. "Doors open by themselves. Heads chase you around. Dead old ladies turn into eight-year-old girls."

The kid just shrugged and strutted over to a little bed tucked away in the corner. "That's Abadazad, for you."

"Abadazad," I said, dusting myself off. "This is so totally weird. I mean, I still can't believe I'm really here."

"Well," the kid replied, plopping down on the bed and grabbing hold of what looked like a stuffed bear, "y'BETTER believe it . . . 'cause I think you're gonna BE here for a while."

I looked at him sitting there, clutching that bear, his little feet tucked up under him, and all of a sudden (don't laugh!) I was sure that it WAS Matt. I mean, it made sense, didn't it?

Queen Ija knew I'd come to Abadazad to find my brother, and she WAS the Greatest Sorceress Ever, and who says she couldn't just cast some super-deluxe spell or twitch her nose and—Presto!—scoop Saint Matt right out of Lanky Manor? Maybe the whole deal with the Rocket Heads was just a joke. (Not a very FUNNY one.) A way to get me into this room— and find out that my brother had been in Inconceivable all along.

I didn't want to just come out and say what I was thinking. I mean, if it really WAS Matty, why ruin the surprise? So I tried to act really casual . . . like I could have cared less (which is hard to do when your heart's slamming around in your chest, and you're so excited you want to jump up and down and squeal like a hyperactive monkey) . . . and I asked: "Who ARE you, kid?"

He waited a couple of seconds, almost like he was trying to build up the suspense . . . and then his thumb burst into flame. Yeah, you read that right. One instant it was a perfectly normal finger and the next it was all lit up like a Fourth of July sparkler. That was strange enough—but then the kid put that burning thumb to the top of his head and SET IT ON FIRE. The whole room was suddenly blazing with light and, pretty quickly, I realized three things:

1) It wasn't his head he lit up, it was some kind of rope, sticking RIGHT OUT OF HIS SCALP. No, not a rope: a wick. A candlewick.

2) The kid (whose clothes, by the way, were even more ridiculous than his shoes. He looked like Buster Brown on a really bad day) was MADE OUT OF WAX.

Yeah, you read THAT right, too: wax. Melting and bubbling down the sides of his head.

3) This DEFINITELY wasn't Matty.

Then Wax-Boy flashed me this lopsided grin . . . more overbite than lip . . . blew out his thumb and announced: "Master Wix—at your service!"

My jaw hit the floor. You'd think that, after everything I'd seen since arriving in Abadazad, I'd be getting used to this kind of weirdoramic stuff, but let me tell you something: you NEVER get used to it. "Master Wix?" I repeated.

"The one and only!" he exclaimed.

I think I mentioned once that Master Wix

was my brother's Absolute Favorite Abadazad Character. Not mine, though: I always thought the kid was kind of pathetic. (Franklin Davies must've felt the same way 'cause he only used Wix in two books . . . which makes him WAY smarter than the morons who made the Abadazad movies. They had Wix as the main character in *Abadazad Five*. Which explains why there was never an *Abadazad SIX*.) I mean, here's this kid—who's not a kid, he's an enchanted candle—who spends all his time searching for his parents. Even when people explain to him that he wasn't born, he was MOLDED IN A FACTORY, the dummy keeps right on looking. And believing that he'll find them.

I dunno. Maybe Matty was a lot like Master Wix. Not that HE was dumb. No way. It's just that, after Dad left, Matt never gave up hoping that Herbert the Great would make some Grand Return. "He'll be back for my birthday," he'd say. Or "I know he'll be home for Christmas." Or Easter. Or Groundhog Day.

Nothing I said—and, believe me, I said plenty—could stop my brother from wishing and hoping. Guess he figured if a lump of wax could act like a living, breathing boy—then why couldn't a lump like Herbert the Great get a sudden burst of the guilts and come running home?

Anyway, Wix trotted over to me, dragging his stuffed animal (which turned out not to be a bear at all but a battered, lumpy dragon). He grabbed my hand in his waxy paw, shook it, and said, "I know I'm supposed t'bow when I meet people—at least that's what Professor Headstrong keeps TELLIN' me—but every time I do, I end up splittin' my pants." Then he laughed, kind of like a donkey with asthma. And, I couldn't help it, I laughed, too.

You ever meet someone and like them—
REALLY like them—instantly? That's what
happened with Wix. Soon as I shook the kid's
hand it felt like he was an old friend that I'd
known . . . well, forever. Or maybe longer. He
didn't seem anywhere near as annoying as he did
in the books. Come to think of it, he didn't look
much like Arthur Pierson's drawings, either—but
then, neither did anybody ELSE I'd run into.

"Nice to meet you, Master Wix," I said. "I'm
Kate."

"I know," he answered. "Martha told me all
about you."

I gave the place a good once-over and
realized we were in some kind of library. A
pretty small one, too. In Brooklyn, we've got
this humongoid library over at Grand Army Plaza,
and I hang out there almost every Saturday.
Each week I find a new book and park myself
in a corner till the librarian tosses me out.
Frances—who subscribes to a thousand
magazines but wouldn't be caught dead reading
an actual book—thinks this is abnormal behavior.
"You need to be with OTHER PEOPLE," she says.
"You need to make FRIENDS." Yeah, like cruising
the mall with those phonies and two-faces from

school would make me socially acceptable.

ANYWAY . . . Wix started telling me that this was Queen Ija's Royal Library, and every book ever written—and every book that WILL be written—in the history of Abadazad was on those shelves.

"What are you talking about?" I said. "Abadazad is like, a QUADRILLION years old. There's maybe a few hundred books in here. No way this can—"

Wix cut me off with that donkey laugh of his, yanking a pair of glasses—round, thick-framed, and covered with waxy thumbprints—out of his pocket. "Try these," he said, handing them to me. I told him I didn't wear glasses, but he just shoved them over the bridge of my nose and, when he did—

All those shelves that'd looked perfectly normal a moment before were suddenly stretching about a A HUNDRED MILES straight up. There must've been MILLIONS of books rising into—well, into Forever.

I kept flipping the glasses back and forth, watching the stacks shrink and rise, shrink and rise. "Sweet!" I said, finally giving the glasses back. I looked over at that little bed in the corner. "And you live here?"

"Yep," Wix replied, scaling a tower of books and reaching up to the shelves. "Ain't it great? I can't really read—Professor's been trying to teach me for longer than I can remember, but I can't seem t'get it . . . so mostly I just look at the pictures."

He grabbed a fat encyclopedia—*The Collected Wisdom of Cogitos Headstrong, S.A.O.J. A. E.S. (Supreme Authority On Just About Every Subject), Part Six Hundred and Seventy-Three*—and plopped himself down on top of the pile. "I love books," he said, and you could tell by how he said it that he really did. "The way they feel. Even the way they smell." He opened the encyclopedia, shoved his nose right in the middle, and took a deep sniff. Then he looked up at me, and I could tell he was embarrassed. "If . . . ah . . . you know what I mean."

"Hey," I answered, "I'm a book-sniffer from WAY back." Wix grinned when I said that. Happy to find someone as weird as he was, I guess. And y'know what? I was happy, too. "The older and moldier the better. You take a snort and it's like you're . . . I dunno . . . breathing in Time. Like you're a part of every person who's ever read it."

I told him that the Abadazad books Matty and I used to read together belonged to my dad when he was little, and how maybe they belonged to his mother before that. (I don't know for sure, because Nana Lizabeth died before I was born and Herbert didn't talk about her much. Maybe he felt the same way about HIS mom that I feel about him.)

"Sometimes," I said, "I'd keep one of those old books on my pillow at night . . ."

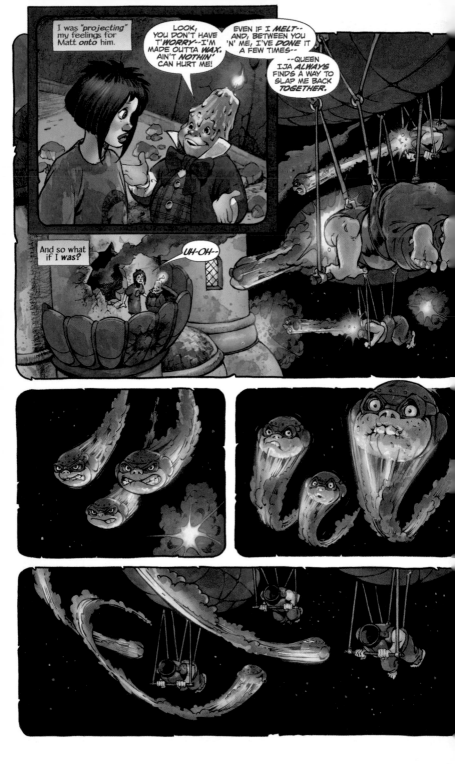

routed, when the gateway to the capital city would be flung open, and she, Aji the Exiled, would, at long last, ascend to the throne that her hated sister had usurped so long ago. Why, then, was there no joy in this moment? Why, then, did she feel like rushing to the dungeon where Ija was jailed, flinging herself at her sister's feet and begging for forgiveness?

"Have you learned, my daughter," a voice behind Aji intoned, rich with a deep and inconsolable sorrow, "that victory is not so sweet as you imagined?"

Aji whirled, her face hardening into a rictus of spite and loathing. "No," she hissed, "not sweet at all. But necessary."

The Floating Warlock drifted up toward the Levitating Tent, his silver hair, grown well past his waist, trailing behind him like the sails of a great ship. Even now, it was impossible for Aji to tell if she was facing a ghost or a man. Perhaps, she thought, her father had always been both or, more probably, neither. Perhaps he was something so different from other beings that it was as fruitless for her to try to understand him as it was for the warriors below to combat

Queen Ija thumbed through the book with a disgusted expression (kind of like Frances when she looks at my report card). "I'm afraid," the Queen said—and I could tell she was trying to choose her words carefully—"that was another of Mr. Davies's . . . embellishments."

"You mean," I gasped, "he MADE IT UP?"

"Precisely," she answered.

"But how can you TRUST a writer who makes things up?"

With an annoyed little wave, Ija poofed the

book away in a spray of stars and fairy dust. I turned to Little Martha, who knew Franklin O. Davies better than anyone in Abadazad, and asked her why he'd DO something like that.

Martha didn't answer. She just sighed—more like the old lady I knew in Brooklyn than the little girl I know here—and looked over at Ija.

The Fairy Queen nodded (it seemed like the two of them did most of their talking without words) and said, "There was a war in your world . . . a very terrible war, as I understand it."

Martha spoke up then—although her voice was barely above a whisper: "The First World War, Your Majesty."

Queen Ija's eyes suddenly flashed with anger (and, believe me, it wasn't an anger you'd ever want to get too close to. Martha told me later that fairies don't get mad very often—and Ija less often than most—but when they do, you'd better run for cover) . . . but a few seconds later, it was replaced by a sadness so deep I was afraid I was gonna drown in it. "The first?" she asked, astonished. "There were more?"

"I'm afraid so," Martha whispered.

Ija was quiet for a long time. "Mr. Davies's only son, Caleb," she finally said, "was a soldier in that brutal conflict—and all the poor man's fears and worries about his child's safety . . . and the safety of his nation . . . weighed heavily upon him—so he poured his despair and helplessness into his stories." She looked off into the shadows of the library . . . and it was almost like she was seeing Davies there, alone at his desk, thinking about Caleb. For a second I thought I could see him, too. "There are many who believe that those final tales are Mr. Davies's greatest work." Her voice kind of stuck in her throat. "I am not one of them."

She turned toward me then, and I saw

fairy tears . . . like liquid diamonds . . . trickling from her eyes (all three of them), gliding down her blue cheeks. And—I hope this makes sense—it wasn't like Queen Ija was crying for herself. It was like she was crying for EVERYONE—in her world AND ours.

I couldn't stand to see her like that . . . so I rushed over to Ija's throne. "Please don't cry, Your Majesty," I said.

She closed her Third Eye, but the other two were still staring at me. "Our tears," Ija said, "are important, Kate. Without them—our hearts would burst." She took my hands in hers. "But

you know all about that, don't you? All these years since your brother was taken . . . and you haven't cried nearly enough."

Listen: I'm not big on crying in front of people. Fact is, I don't even like to cry in front of MYSELF. Sure, there've been a few times since my brother disappeared when I let the waterworks go—I can't deny it, right, 'cause you've seen it right here in these pages—but every time I do, I feel kind of stupid. Embarrassed. And weak, I guess. So how come I ended up with my head buried in Ija's lap, blubbering and sobbing, with boogers bubbling out of my nose?

I figure the Queen put a whammy on me . . . y'know, some kind of Weeping Spell to turn the faucet on. I should've been mad about that . . . but I wasn't. I wasn't embarrassed, either. Sure, Wix and Martha were standing just a few feet away, watching me ooze tears and snotballs . . . sure my heart was burning and melting worse than Wax-Boy's head . . . but I knew it was okay.

More than okay: it was right. I NEEDED

to let it out in a way I never had before. Y'know how Ija was crying for the whole world? Well, it felt like I was crying for my whole FAMILY. For Matty, Frances, Gramma Esther. Even for Deadbeat Herbert. (Although I'm still not sure why.) Crying for everything we'd been through together. And everything we'd lost.

I cried for what felt like ten thousand years, and then, just to be safe, cried for five thousand more. Then, when there were no tears left, I wiped my nose on my shirt and picked up my head. "Your . . . Your Majesty," I sniffled. "Will you help me find him? Will you help me get Matt back?"

She ran her hands through my hair—all three of those eyes open now—and said, "Of course I will, Kate. We just need a little time before—"

Soon as I heard those words "a little time" I went totally ballistic. (Scary, isn't it, how we can go from one mood to another in just a second?) All of a sudden Ija wasn't The Fairy Queen of Abadazad—she was Just Another Stupid Grown-up like my dumb parents and my dumb teachers. All they EVER did was tell me how what I thought, what I felt, what I wanted to do was WRONG . . . and if I just had some patience and waited a little while, everything would get better. Only, it NEVER got better. It always turned into a bigger disaster than before. Grown-ups were idiots, and I was sick of them all. So sick I could puke.

"Time?" I shouted, pushing myself to my

feet. "I haven't seen my brother since I was NINE YEARS OLD! We've got to do something NOW!"

Ija didn't seem to mind the fact that I was shrieking in her face like the lead singer from Thrashing Plague. She just nodded her head and said, "That's exactly what the Lanky Man wants. He sent his Rocket Heads to stir you to rash action—and he'd be delighted if you set off for the Wretchedly Awful City before you've been fully prepared."

I stormed across the room. "Yeah, well," I howled (it's amazing I wasn't foaming at the mouth), "at least HE'S doing something— which is more than I can say for YOU!"

Martha sucked in her breath, like she'd never heard anyone talk to Queen Ija that way. "Kate!" she called out. "Kate—don't!"

"Leave me alone!" I yelled, yanking the door open.

Only, the door yanked back. Hard.

And slammed itself.

I knew it was Ija's doing so I whirled around. "Knock off the mumbo jumbo," I screamed, "and let me OUT of here!"

The Queen came soaring across the

library on her winged throne and stopped a couple of inches in front of me, hovering there in the air. "I'll say it again, Kate. Walk out of this room and you'll be doing EXACTLY what the Lanky Man wants." She waved her hand toward the door, and it popped open. "No more . . . mumbo jumbo," she said. "Go. If that's what you truly desire."

I looked from Ija to the open door and back again. I folded my arms across my chest. I tapped my foot. I gave her the Patented Jameson Glare.

But I didn't leave.

Because the truth is Queen Ija WASN'T like my parents and my teachers. She wasn't like any person, grown-up or kid, that I'd ever met. I knew the Queen really cared about me and my brother . . . knew she'd do everything in her power to get Matty back. And if she was telling me to wait—well, maybe there was a good reason for it, and maybe—JUST THIS ONE TIME—it wouldn't hurt to actually listen to an adult. Besides, Ija was supposed to be something like fifty thousand years old. You've gotta figure that, by their fifty thousandth birthday, grown-ups start making SOME kind of sense.

Y'know, I think the real reason I got so mad at her (and, really, I'm just figuring this out right now) was because I could. Because I knew that, no matter how big a tantrum I threw, how much of a First-Class Brat I acted like . . . she'd still love me.

That sounds funny, doesn't it? I mean, I'd only just met her, but I absolutely knew that Ija loved me . . . in a way nobody'd ever loved me before. It's not that I was anything so special— if you've been reading this far, it's pretty clear that I'm not—it's that . . . well . . . Ija just LOVED.

It was Who She Was. If the Lanky Man himself would have walked into that Throne Room, she would have loved him the same. Even if she was angry or disappointed or upset, it wouldn't matter. That love would always be there.

I'm not big on apologies—just ask my mother—but you can bet I was ready to get down on my knees and grovel like a pro. Before I could open my mouth, though, the Queen did this thing with her hands—swept one open palm across the other like she was wiping away every stupid and hurtful thing I'd ever done—and said, "Forgiven . . . and forgotten!" And when she said it, I could tell that she really meant it. Not like most people who PRETEND they forgive you . . . but you know, deep down, they're still holding a grudge. ~~I hope Matty forgives me that easily when I find him. I hope he~~

"Now," Ija announced, "I want you and Martha to go back to your rooms, freshen up—and prepare for the party."

"What party?" I asked.

"Why, the WELCOMING party."

"Who are you welcoming?"

"You, of course!"

My jaw hit the floor again (funny how often that was happening). "You mean—like in the books?"

Martha came rushing over to me. "Just like the books," she squealed. "Only better!"

Almost every Abadazad book either began or ended with an absolutely killer party. When Little Martha returned to Inconceivable after a few months away (in the beginning of the series she'd go back and forth between worlds. After her father, Colonel Cooper, died—in Book Six—she moved into the Royal Palace permanently): there was a party. When Martha and her friends saved the Capital City from some enemy like the Lanky Man, the Lotus Floaters, or the Merciless Mind-Foggers: there was a party. When Mary Annette and the Balloonicorn set out to find the Pipe Dreamer's Imagilodious Flute: party. When Mr. Gloom fell down a hole and accidentally discovered the Underground Land of the Puffy Pale People: party. When—

Well, I think you get the idea: Queen Ija

LOVED parties. Gigantor bashes that went on for days (sometimes weeks!). Every character that was ever in the books would show up (and, if they weren't mentioned in the actual story, Arthur Pierson managed to squeeze them into one of the illustrations). There was enough food to feed every single citizen of Inconceivable (and they were all invited, too). The Singing Swami—who, with his ten arms, was a one-man orchestra—played his Cosmic Symphonies, and everyone would dance—usually about fifteen feet off the floor (the Swami's music tended to make people levitate)—doing the Warlock Waltz or the Ija Glide, as the sun set over the Enchanted Gardens.

I figured if Ija actually wanted to throw some big shebang in MY HONOR, it'd be impolite to say no, right? Especially after the way I'd already acted. I'm not much of a party girl back home, because A) I almost never get asked to any, and B) when I do get invited it's usually by some total loser, and why would I want to go to a party filled with jerks like me? But I figured this might be kinda/sorta fun. (Okay, okay—truth is, I

was so excited I thought I was gonna levitate WITHOUT the Singing Swami's help.) So I told Ija sure, I'd go to her party IF we could discuss our plans for rescuing Matty right after it was over. The Queen said that sounded perfect to her, so Little Martha and I said good-bye and headed back to our rooms.

"Hey!" I realized as we were walking down the hall. "What happened to Wix?"

"That boy," Martha said, rolling her eyes, "has got wax ants in his pants. He can never stay in one place very long. He's always running off, getting himself into trouble."

"I don't know," I said. "He seems like a sweet kid t'me."

"And who says troublemakers can't be sweet?" Martha asked—and I could tell by the way she said it that she wasn't talking about Wix, she was talking about ME. Which was a compliment. I think.

This was my first chance to ask Martha why she hadn't been in her room when I went looking for her during the R-Head attack. I didn't say how worried I'd been— figured it would only make her feel bad—but

I think she could kind of tell.

Turns out she was with Queen Ija and the Veiled Vizier (Ija's right-hand man. Or woman. No one really knows who's behind the veil) the whole time, playing Jaijai Jumpers. (Jaijai's a city in southern Abadazad, overlooking the Ocean of Light, and Jumpers is a game kind of like checkers, only the pieces are alive, and they don't always do what you tell them to.)

"Playing Jumpers—in the middle of the night?"

"I've been wrestling with insomnia," Martha told me, "for a long time now. Happens when you get up there in years, y'know. And even though I'm a girl again . . . I'm still sleeping like an old lady."

Pretty soon we were back in my apartment. We talked for a little while—which was nice, because I really haven't had anyone to talk to at night since Matty . . . but we were both so pooped after being up for so long that we decided to call it quits.

Martha gave me a big hug and a wet kiss on the cheek (for the record: I HATE hugging, and kissing makes me totally GAG . . . I haven't let Frances kiss me since I was, like, seven or eight . . . but for some dumb reason I let Martha do it. I used to let Matty do it, too . . . but, hey,

Matty's MATTY, after all) and told me she'd be by later to pick me up for the party . . . then ran down the hall to her apartment.

I almost ran after her. All of a sudden, I had this dumb idea that maybe Martha'd want to stay over. Not 'cause I was afraid of sleeping alone or anything, but because I thought it'd be, y'know, kinda fun. (Back home, I don't think I EVER had a friend sleep over at my house. Of course the fact that I didn't HAVE any friends might have had something to do with it.) I decided not to ask her, though. I mean, it really WAS a Majorly Dumb idea, right?

So here I sit, writing in my enchanted diary (or journal or memoirs or WHATEVER this is), trying to catch up on everything that's happened. Now that I know we're going after my brother soon, I want to make sure I get every little detail down. Saint Matt's missed a lot, and I figure we can snuggle up at bedtime like we used to and I can read this to him.

Not just read it—SHOW him. Just flip through the pages, Matty, and watch Kate Jameson's Magical 3D Reality Show. Amazing, huh? But it's also kind of brain damaging . . . y'know, watching yourself running around INSIDE THE PAGES OF A BOOK and actually LISTENING TO YOURSELF TALK? It's bad enough that my nose looks ten times fatter than it is, but my voice is SO not squeaky, and I do NOT have a Brooklyn accent. (I wonder if the book's trying to mess with me? But that would mean the diary's alive or something. Which is MUCH too creepy to contemplate.)

And what about the Lanky Man and his little disciples? (Who ARE those kids anyway . . . and how come they follow Lanks around like puppies?)

And MATT.

I guess it's a good thing that I can see my brother again after all these years . . . but can you imagine how it makes me feel when I see poor Matty STUFFED IN A BOTTLE and hooked up to that disgusting machine? No, you CAN'T. Because it isn't YOUR fault that he's there. Because

Anyway, I'm gonna close my eyes for a couple of minutes—I'm WASTED all of a sudden—and then, I guess . . .

YARRRRHHHHHH...!!!

New entry. A lot's happened since the last time I wrote...

. . . but in order to get to where I am NOW (which is pretty much smack in the Middle of Nowhere), I've gotta start from where I was THEN.

Which was where, exactly? Oh, yeah:

So there I was in the Royal Palace, sound asleep in my room. After that awful dream— which I pretty much think was a lot MORE than a dream—about Matty, I slept like death. I probably would have KEPT sleeping for hours, too, except that some idiot started poking me in the ribs and telling me to "Get up, darlin', or you'll be late!"

At first, I figured it was Frances (who's transformed dragging me out of bed into an art form). "I don't care if I'm late," I mumbled, pushing her away, rolling over, and slamming a pillow over my head. "I hate school and school hates me—now leave me alone."

"First of all," said a voice that was so hideously cheerful I knew right away it couldn't POSSIBLY be my mother, "if that's the way you talk to your mama, you should hang your head in shame! Second of all, I agree that school is an utter waste of time! Third of all—" And then Miss Cheerful grabbed the sheets, yanking them—and me—right onto the floor. "—life's too short to be spent in bed!"

Tumbling onto my butt—which was still pretty sore from being bounced around by the Rocket Heads—was enough to wake me right up and remind me that this wasn't the Jameson dump in Brooklyn, it was the Royal Palace in Inconceivable. So who, I wondered, was the twittering, rib-poking moron that wrecked my sleep?

But the thing is . . . it wasn't a who. It was a WHAT.

It was a DRESS.

No lie: there was a dress (that looked like it was cobbled together from a dozen different patterns—flowers, polka dots, paisleys, swirls—with colors so bright you could get a migraine just looking at them) standing over me. And, no, it wasn't on a hanger. It wasn't on ANYTHING. It was just floating there in midair . . . flapping its arms at me. Then there were these striped gloves hovering on either side of the dress—one of 'em was clutching an umbrella and waving it in my direction—and, drifting a few inches above the neckline, a pair of thick glasses. Topping it all off was this TRULY grotesque hat, with so many roses and daffodils on it you'd think it was grown instead of sewn.

The dress started swishing closer, aiming that umbrella straight at me like a sword and chirping "Up! Up! UP!" in a voice so sweet I was afraid I was gonna go into sugar shock. I was so totally freaked (and don't act so superior, you'd feel the same way if an umbrella-wielding dress attacked YOU) that I ducked behind the bed. "Back off, dress!" I hollered. (That's as stupid to write as it was to say.) "I'm a personal friend of Queen Ija's and—"

The dress laughed and said, "Of course you are, darlin'! And any friend of my niece is a friend of mine!"

I stuck my head out a little. "Your niece?"

The gloves put the umbrella down, grabbed hold of the edges of the skirt, and the whole dress kind of crinkled and curtsied. "Great Auntie Nott," the dress chirped, "at your service!"

"Auntie Who?"

"No, no, no," the dress said, plopping down on the bed. "Great Auntie Hu is vacationing in the Green Desert with the Sprouting

Sorceress. I'm Great Auntie NOTT."

I was beginning to think that maybe she (it?) wasn't trying to murder me with that umbrella, so I inched onto the bed next to it (her?).

"So," I said, "you're Ija's aunt?"

"Not a blood aunt, mind you. More of an HONORARY one—which, when you think about it, is even better. She CHOSE me. And, believe me, it's not often we get to choose our families."

"But," I said, a little reluctant to bring it up, "you're not—"

"That's right. I'm Nott. Auntie Nott." The glasses leaned in toward me, with that horrendous hat close behind. "Now, why don't we—"

"No, no . . ." I said, backing away a little. "What I mean is, you're not in the BOOKS."

"Actually, Mr. Davies DID put me in one of them—a very substantial part, too—but I'm afraid his editor cut me out." One of those striped gloves fluttered in front of my face. "Oh well," she said (and she really didn't seem to mind), "that's life in the literary world!"

"Well, I think it stinks," I said. "You'd make a fantastic character . . . y'know, being a living dress and all."

"A dress?" Nott sounded surprised. "Kate, Kate, Kate—just because you can't SEE a person doesn't mean they're not THERE."

"You mean . . . you aren't a dress?"

One of those sleeves wrapped itself around my shoulders and—MAJORLY weird—I could feel an actual arm through the material.

"Once," Nott said, "I was a girl, not all that different from you. But I was so shy, darlin'— it was painful. I couldn't bear to face other people. Even looking at myself in the mirror gave me a case of the shakes."

"But why?" I asked.

"Who can say for sure? All I know is . . . from the moment I drew my first breath, life simply terrified me."

I almost told her that it terrified ME, too, sometimes . . . but you don't just go saying things like that to people . . . or dresses . . . you don't really know. "And so I decided to hide myself away in my room. Wouldn't speak to my parents . . . my brothers and sisters. Nobody. My poor mama and papa tried and tried to coax me out—but it was just no use."

"I dunno," I said, thinking about it. "Hiding out in your room sounds like a pretty good plan t'me. You can read books, watch TV, do all kinds of—"

For the first time Auntie Nott let a hint of sadness creep into her voice. "Hiding from life," she said, "is NEVER a good plan."

"Why? What happened?"

"Well . . . eventually . . . after years and years of living like I was invisible, I just started to . . . fade away. Little bits of me at first. So little I never even noticed. But then one morning I woke up . . . AND I WAS GONE."

"Gone? Just like that?"

"Just like that," she cooed, getting so close I could smell her breath (which was a little like cotton candy). "And there was nothing anybody could do to help me."

"But there are so many magicians around here that SOMEBODY must've been able to—"

"Magic's a very personal thing, Kate," Auntie Nott said. "And this was a spell I'd created in the deeps of my own heart." She sighed—kind of like a harp tinkling. "So here I am. Or should I say—here I'm not!"

She started laughing again—which really confused me. "I don't get it," I said. "That's a terrible story . . . but you don't seem upset at all. In fact, you—"

"Now, THAT was the curious thing!" Auntie Nott exclaimed, jumping up off the bed, grabbing me by the wrists, and spinning me around in circles so fast I thought I was gonna hurl. "The moment I became invisible, my shyness simply evaporated! And my love of people . . . of life . . . came shooting up out of me like red-hot lava from a volcano!"

Then she started singing—"Joy, joy, joy!"—like some deranged Mary Poppins, finally letting me go and sending me staggering across the room, tripping over a table and crashing down onto my butt again. (There wasn't much more my poor cheeks could take.) "Joy in everything! And that," Nott went on, rustling over and helping me up, "is why you can't sleep the day away. The party . . . YOUR party . . . is going to start soon—and it's time to make you even more beautiful than you already are!"

"Beautiful?" I squeaked (okay, so maybe the diary was right about that). "Me? No offense but . . . did your BRAINS disappear along with the REST of you?"

Nott ignored that and started gliding in circles around me. "You certainly can't go in THAT thing," she humphed, pointing at my Thrashing Plague T-shirt.

"Hey," I said defensively, "with your taste in clothes I wouldn't go around passing judgment. And besides, I didn't exactly have time t'change when the Blue Globe zapped me here."

"Not to worry, darlin'," Nott answered. "I always come prepared." She floated across the room and opened one of the closet doors. It was empty inside—at least until Nott aimed her umbrella and shot out a blast of light that was almost as blinding as her dress.

When I could finally see again, the closet was FULL. Stuffed with, like, a hundred gowns so gaudy and frilly that not even Miss America would be caught dead in them. "Well, don't just stand there," Nott insisted—

Funny. Standing there, staring at myself in the mirror (which isn't something I normally do, unless, y'know, I'm trying to pop a zit or something), I kind of SAW my mom and my gramma. I don't mean in a vision or anything. I mean, they were there IN ME. I guess I never noticed that before. How, in some weird way, the three of us are all a part of each other.

You know how much I loved my Gramma Esther, so the idea of being a part of her was really sweet. But Frances? Usually when she points out something the two of us do alike, I get totally annoyed, say something obnoxious, and change the subject (no kid on the planet wants to be like their parents, right?) . . . but right then, I didn't mind it. In fact—and don't ask me to explain it 'cause I can't—I kind of LIKED the idea.

Which got me wondering about Frances and maybe/kinda/sorta WORRYING about her, too. I mean, what's gonna happen when she wakes up in the morning and finds out that I'm gone? (Or maybe she ALREADY woke up. Time's so screwy in Abadazad, it's hard to tell if I've been here for a couple of seconds, a couple of days, or a couple of years.) She's gonna think I ran away (which, let's be honest, I've done before . . . although, let's be honest, I've never gotten very far. Where was I gonna go? Out to visit my father? If I showed up at Herbert the Great's house, he'd probably slam the door in my face. Yeah—if he even RECOGNIZED me).

Considering what a nervous wreck my mother is, she'll probably put posters up all over the neighborhood (and I bet she'll use one of those awful pictures from Cousin Jeanette's wedding, too). Or maybe she'll just freak out and lock herself in the bedroom with a bottle, the way she did after Matty disappeared.

Want to hear something supremely dumb? I kind of missed Frances then. I kind of miss her NOW. I know it sounds ridiculous . . . missing someone who drives you crazy and screws up all the time and is maybe the Worst Mother Ever. But, hey, I drive HER crazy and I screw up even more, and if there was an award for Worst Daughter I'm sure I'd win it, hands down. Which I guess means we're a pretty good match.

"LOOK at you, Kate!"

I spun around, and Little Martha was there . . .

dressed up even
fancier than I was
and looking twice
as pretty. We
both started
dancing around,
showing off
our dresses
and giggling like,
well, a couple
of girls. (And,
really, I've never
thought of myself
as a girl. Well, not one
of those GIRLY girls, anyway. I've always just
thought of myself as Kate.) It was idiotic, I
know, but it was fun (and it got my mind off
Frances, too).

Auntie Nott just floated in a circle
around us, clucking like a mother hen. "The
two loveliest creatures I've ever seen.
Now, come on," she said, swishing toward
the door, "the party's about to start."

"Now?"

"Don't you hear the music?" Martha said.
And as soon as she said it, I did. Some of it

sounded familiar—like bits and pieces of Beethoven (Saint Matt's favorite. What can I tell you? The kid's not normal), the Beatles (Frances still has a crush on John Lennon and the guy's been dead for, like, a hundred years), Frank Sinatra (who I only know about 'cause Gramma Esther used to play his stuff all the time), and Thrashing Plague all mixed up in a blender. But some of it was like nothing I'd ever heard before: mysterious instruments and magical voices that made you want to laugh, cry, dance, run in circles, stand on your head, and bark like a dog . . . all at the same time!

"Is that . . . the Singing Swami?" I asked.

"It is," Great Auntie Nott replied. "And he's playing JUST FOR YOU."

Martha grabbed my hand and started pulling me across the room. "Come on, Kate! Oh, I can't wait to introduce you to Professor Headstrong and Mary Annette and the Balloonicorn and—"

I pulled my hand away. "NO!" I yelped.

"What is it, darlin'?" Auntie Nott asked.

"What's wrong?" What I WANTED to say was "I've never been so excited in my life and I've never been so freaked and I HATE crowds and I can't WAIT to meet all these people I've been reading about since I was born and this is all so overwhelming that I think I'm gonna explode like a ROCKET HEAD!" But all that came out was: "Can I . . . ah . . . can I have a minute here?"

Martha just smiled—I could tell she understood—and said, "We'll be waiting right outside for you, sweetheart."

After they left, I took a few deep breaths (well, maybe a few thousand), straightened my dress, fussed with my hair, went to the bathroom (twice. I pee a LOT when I'm nervous), took a few thousand more deep breaths, and—

"Now, ain't you the fancy one?" I recognized that voice and . . . sure enough . . . when I looked in the mirror I saw Master Wix behind me, sitting on a tabletop.

"Wixy!" I said, spinning around. "How'd you get in here?"

"This joint's loaded with secret passageways. The Floating Warlock used 'em all the time so he could come and go without anyone noticin'. I don't even think the Queen knows about most of 'em—" He gave me a wink and flashed that lopsided smile of his. "—but I do."

"Well, I'm glad you're back. You can come down to the party with me and—"

He hopped off the table. "Not goin'," he said.

"What do you MEAN you're not going?"

Wix got this strange look on his face. Like he was, I dunno, disappointed in me or something. "Hey, it's none o' my business," he said.

"Tell me."

He looked down at the floor, fiddling with his stuffed dragon, then looked up and said, "Kate—I been searchin' for my mom 'n' dad for as long as I can remember. An' I'm gonna go on searchin' . . . no matter what anybody says."

Five years.

"Family . . . family's all we got."

I hadn't seen my brother in FIVE YEARS.

"You can't wait around."

And there I was, looking like Rapunzel with a haircut . . . going to a party where people'd be laughing and dancing like life was some happy little dream. How could I DO that when my brother was in the Wretchedly Awful City, locked away in Lanky Manor, stuffed like some lab rat in a bottle of . . . WHATEVER that green gunk was?

"Y'gotta go after Matt right now."

Sure, Queen Ija meant well. But Matty wasn't HER brother, he was MINE. He wasn't depending on HER, he was depending on ME.

"An' I wanna go with you!"

Can you believe that it took some half-witted kid made out of wax to bring me to my senses? "Okay," I said to Wixy. "Let's blow this dump."

I wanted to tell Martha what I was doing, but I knew she'd try to talk me out of it . . . so I took one last look in the mirror, then ducked into the bathroom and changed back into my T-shirt (I wasn't gonna go stomping across half of Abadazad in a ball gown and heels, was I?). Then we crawled out through a tunnel hidden in the back of the fireplace.

"Awfully dark in here," I whispered. "You sure this is the way out?"

"Hey," Wix answered, "I ain't never been wrong yet!"

We wriggled along for like twenty minutes . . . my knees got all scraped up, my arms were getting cramped . . . and then we came to this ledge that dropped off into the biggest blackest Nothing I'd ever seen.

"Now what?" I asked, afraid of the answer.

"NOW," Wix said—

When I was just a little squirt...back in those ancient days before *Saint Matt* was born...my dead-beat father took me to see *Pinocchio*.

I hate to admit it -- but most of the junk I watched back then had brain-damaged *hand puppets* or fuzzy *purple dinosaurs* in them.

So here's the first movie I ever see on the big screen (and when you're four years old, the operative word is *big*), and it's scaring me half to *death*. Not that I'm gonna admit it to *Herbert the Great*. We get through *most* of it without me screaming or fainting.

Then that *humongous whale* shows up.

...one look at that ugly fish and started screaming and crying-- and then, for good measure...

...threw up in my father's popcorn

Get the *picture?*

and, best of all, listening to the Wubbtales' sublime songs and Uncle Waterlogged's preposterous jokes.

The Waterlogged Warlock loved a good joke, and he had spent several thousand years traversing the Kingdom (and numerous adjacent worlds) compiling what he called "The Cosmic Compendium of Humor." (This, of course, offended Professor Headstrong terribly. "There is no place," he often sniffed, "in life for humor. Time wasted in frivolous pursuits would be far better spent in study!" Uncle Waterlogged always laughed uproariously when Headstrong said this, which offended the Professor all the more!)

Ija commanded her chair to sail across the room, settling just beside the bowl. She tapped on the glass gently, sending the dear little Wubbtales scattering in panic; but the old man snored on. The Queen, a look of subversive delight on her face, then removed her wand from the folds of her robe, waving it three times and whispering several words in Old Zadish. The Scarlet Globe at the wand's tip began to glow a fiery red and the Waterlogged Warlock immediately began to rise, ever so slowly, from his sandy bed, floating up

The Scarlet Globe at the wand's tip began to glow a fiery red.

. . . but this guy? (Fish?) (Whatever.) Major-league creepy. Except—and here's the really weird part—he WASN'T.

Don't get me wrong, I was scared—really scared—but there was something . . . familiar about him. Y'know that feeling you get when, all of a sudden, right in the middle of the day, you remember an old dream? How it all comes rushing back and you can't believe you ever forgot it? Well, that's the feeling I had when I looked at him. (It?) (Whatever.) Like I'd dreamed him once . . . a long, LONG time ago.

"And what is your name, child?" Fish-Guy asked, the purple jewel in his staff getting brighter with every word . . . then fading down a little when he was done talking.

"Kate," I said . . . choking the word out.

Fish-Guy waved us closer—so I grabbed Wix's hand and took a couple of steps toward him. I figured he was gonna SMELL kinda fishy. And he did, too. But he also smelled like the ocean on the greatest beach day ever.

"Kate what?" he insisted.

"Jameson," I gulped. "Kate Jameson."

"Indeed you ARE," he said.

"Wait a minute! You know who I am?"

"As intimately as I know myself."

"Then . . . uh . . . how come you asked me my—"

He sat back in his chair—I guess it was more like a throne—and tilted his head to one side (which made all this water run out of his ear).

"Names," he said, "have POWER, Kate—and it's important to always speak your own out clearly, and with pride. If you don't, you just might forget who you are." He smiled. I think.

Hard to tell with that bizarro mouth of his. "I know that sounds absurd—but the fact is, people forget themselves all the time. Why," he went on, "it even happened to ME once. Utterly lost myself—and spent a hundred years adrift . . . in the Ocean of Nothing."

"A hundred years adrift . . . ?" Something about that sounded SO familiar . . . and then it HIT me: "Book Three!" I whooped. "*The Eight Oceans of Abadazad!*" And all of a sudden I realized who he was: "Oh, my gosh! You're Queen Ija's UNCLE! You're the WATERLOGGED WARLOCK!"

"Indeed I AM!" he roared, kind of like a happy sea lion (okay, so I don't really know what a sea lion sounds like, but I'll BET it sounds just like the Waterlogged Warlock). Then he stood up—must've been seven or eight feet tall—water spurting out the top of his head like a fountain.

Eight Oceans was one of my all-time favorite Abadazad books. I must've read it five times by myself and another five to Matty. That was the only book where the Waterlogged Warlock had a big part. (Usually Davies just stuck him in a few scenes . . .

mainly for laughs. And he WAS pretty funny.)

Y'see, in the story, everyone in the Royal Palace wakes up one morning to discover that Queen Ija is missing . . . and the Warlock leads Little Martha, Mary Annette, Professor Headstrong, Mr. Gloom, and The Balloonicorn on a journey across . . . surprise! . . . the eight oceans of Abadazad searching for her.

The Ocean of Nothing chapter used to scare the spit out of Matt (kinda spooked me, too). I mean, they spend years and years stuck in all this fog and darkness and gooey black rain, not remembering anything . . . including each other. (Matty was sure that that was what happened to Herbert the Great after he moved out. Figured Dear Old Deadbeat got stuck in his own Ocean of Nothing—and that's why he forgot us. I never had the heart to remind Matt that, even when he was living with us, Herbert hardly knew who we were.)

Anyway, Martha and the others eventually break free of the Ocean of Nothing and make their way into the Ocean of Desserts (now, that's my favorite part. I mean, who can't appreciate a forty-foot-tall piece of

chocolate cake?), but the Waterlogged
Warlock falls asleep—which the old guy was
always doing—and gets left behind.

No matter how many times we read
Eight Oceans, Saint Matt used to cry and
cry when that happened—even though he
knew that Uncle Waterlogged would show up
again in the next-to-last chapter, just in
time to save everybody from Sarabinda
the Seer and—

And I'm rambling again, right? Sorry.

So there I was, holding Wixy's hand (but
not too tight. I figure a kid made out of wax
must squish pretty easy), and the Warlock
bends down to grab a book up out of the
water. Weird enough that there WERE books
drifting by with all the fish and seaweed and
junk . . . but what was weirder was that the
book he grabbed was the same one I'd just
been talking about: *The Eight Oceans of
Abadazad!* (Weirder still, I noticed that ALL
the books floating by were Abadazad books.)

The Warlock studied one of Pierson's
illustrations . . . then turned to me with
an odd look in his eyes (well, they were
pretty odd to begin with, but this look was

ODD odd). "Are you surprised," he asked me, "that I don't look like the Waterlogged Warlock in Mr. Davies's books?"

"I guess I SHOULD be surprised," I said, "but I think I'm starting to catch on." I snorted and rolled my eyes. "Franklin O. Davies! Jeez! What a LOSER!"

"Loser?" He sounded confused. Almost hurt.

But Big-Mouth Jameson just plowed right on. "Yeah," I said, "Davies screwed up EVERYTHING about this place. Changed it around so much that—"

So the Warlock makes this big sweeping gesture with his staff . . . and all those Abadazad books come rocketing up out of the water. One of 'em whizzed right over my head.

"Mr. Davies," he said, waving his staff around like an orchestra conductor, making the books whip and whirl through the air, "may have changed the details, Kate . . . but he captured the SOUL of Abadazad. And for that . . . all of us here are forever grateful."

"But he LIED," I said. (Actually, I whined.)

"No," the Warlock insisted. "He simply added HIS formidable imagination to a world that was BORN of imagination. And that, my dear, isn't a lie. That—" All at once the books dropped. Fast. Hitting the water with a tremendous splash. "—is a VERY DEEP TRUTH."

While I was thinking that over (and there was a LOT to think about), the WW looked around with an annoyed expression on his face. "Where," he asked, "is your little friend?"

That's when I realized I wasn't holding Wixy's hand anymore. "Hey! Where'd he go?"

I heard this splishing sound from somewhere deeper in the cave (which . . . I had to keep reminding myself . . . wasn't a cave at all. It was THAT WHALE-THING'S BELLY), and I could just about make Wixy out down there, tiptoeing away. (Where was the dummy going? To hail a cab?)

Next thing I know, the Warlock dives under the water (which is pretty strange, since the water's only like a few inches deep) and two seconds later he comes popping up again . . . right in front of Wix. "YOUR NAME!" he roared.

Well, Wix pretty much froze up. All he could do was say "Uh . . . uh . . . uh . . . uh . . ." again and again. I ran over and scooped the kid up in my arms. "His name's Wix," I said. "Master Wix."

The Warlock just folded his arms across his

chest and stared at me (guess everyone's got their own version of the Patented Jameson Glare). "He must speak it out for himself," he said.

I was scared (I mean, what was with this guy? One minute he seems like your buddy and the next he's ready to bite your head off), but I was MORE scared for Wix. Which I guess is why I had the courage to speak up. "Can't you see he's afraid of you? The poor kid's—"

"For himself," the Warlock repeated, in a whisper that seemed to echo all around us like thunder. Then . . . I wasn't sure . . . but I THINK he winked at me. Maybe, I thought, he's not as angry as he seems.

So I put Wix down and gave him an encouraging look. He clutched his stuffed dragon to his chest—the poor kid was sweating paraffin—and said his name, in the most pathetic little voice I'd ever heard.

"Louder," the Warlock insisted. It took everything the poor kid had—but he tried it again, a little louder this time: "Master Wix."

It was weird. Up in Inconceivable, Wix had pretty much acted like nothing got to him. I mean, this is the kid who laughed at the Rocket Heads. Guess he felt safe under Queen Ija's protection.

But down there, all that tough-guy stuff just . . . melted away. Wax or not—he was just a little boy. And a pretty sweet one, too.

The Warlock got this wild look in his eyes then . . . and yanked Wixy up into the air by his shoulders. I was about three seconds away from throwing myself at the Fish-Guy's feet and begging for mercy, when he started shooting water out of his head again and laughing. "Well DONE, Master Wix! Well DONE!"

Then Wix started laughing, too—more out of relief than anything—and before I knew it, I was joining in. I didn't really understand what had just happened . . . but, looking back, it feels like Uncle Waterlogged was testing Wix somehow. And I guess the kid passed.

Waterlogged hefted Master Wix up onto his shoulder, and the three of us started sploshing along together. "I don't blame the boy for fearing me," he said. "You see, I spend most of my time away from the city . . . deep under the waves . . . dreaming. And when I DO return here, I much prefer the canals beneath Inconceivable to the palace corridors above."

The water was getting deeper as we

walked along . . . it was above my knees . . . and I was starting to wonder where, exactly, he was taking us. "It's understandable, then," the Warlock went on, "that the Inconceivablites would tell . . . exaggerated tales about me. The sad truth is, even in Abadazad, people fear what they don't know."

Wix puffed out his chest like some little tough guy. "Hey, I ain't scared o' you," he said. "I ain't scared o'—"

He never finished the sentence because . . . just then . . . this INCREDIBLE geyser of water came GUSHING up from right under us (Wix started shrieking like a five-year-old girl—and maybe I did, too) . . . sending all three of us barreling straight into the air like surfers riding a tidal wave. We're heading right for the roof (if whales have roofs), and I figure this is it . . . we're gonna smash right into it. But, at the last second, I see that there's some kind of HOLE up there (blowholes, I think they call 'em), and the wave pipes us right through it, and we land . . . on our butts (and you can imagine how THAT felt after all my poor behind had been through?) . . . right on the whale-thing's back.

I figure Monstro's not too happy about this, and I ask the WW to PLEASE get us out of there . . . fast . . . but instead he just struts over to the whale-thing's head, pets it—like it's Benji or something—and says, "Thank you, Mother Pfoughh."

And the whale-thing answers back, in this voice that sounds like a foghorn—if a foghorn were a woman. "De . . . lighted . . . Uncle . . . Water . . . logged," it (she?) says. "We . . . Wubb . . . tales . . . live . . . only . . . to . . . serve . . ."

I couldn't believe what I was hearing. "This—is a WUBBTALE?"

"Certainly," the Warlock said.

"But the books—"

"TRUTH, Kate," the Warlock said, as Mother Pfoughh began to glide forward through the canal, "not DETAILS." A bunch of other Wubbtales . . . smaller ones . . . and younger, too, I think . . . came racing up beside us—slapping their tails against the water and splashing us. Wix seemed annoyed . . . but I kind of liked it.

"Mother," Uncle Waterlogged said, tapping the Wubbtale gently on the head with his

snake-head staff, "if you will . . . ?"

And the big Wubbtale went into a dive, like she was some kind of living submarine or something. "Hey!" I shouted, grabbing on to the Warlock's arm. "HEY—what're you trying t'do—DROWN us?"

The weird thing is, I said those last couple of words WHILE WE WERE UNDER WATER. And not only was I talking down there . . . I was BREATHING, too!

"No need to panic," the Warlock said, pointing to the glowing gem at the top of his staff. "The magic of the Purple Globe will protect you."

Of course, the stories never said anything about a PURPLE Globe, just Martha's Blue Globe (y'know, the one that moved people from our world to Abadazad) and Queen Ija's Scarlet one (which was this all-purpose gizmo that could pretty much do anything Franklin O. Davies needed it to). I should've been annoyed, right? Here was another one that Frankie-boy screwed up. But I guess I was beginning to understand what the Warlock meant about truth and details. I mean, there are just some things that are bigger than words.

And that's what I saw down there, miles and miles beneath the Inconceivable Canals: something totally beyond words. I'll try to describe it for you—and I hope maybe the magic of the diary will help you see. And understand.

There were ruins . . . ENTIRE CITIES . . . each one floating in a glistening water bubble . . . rolling gently along the water currents. And each city felt—I wanna say ancient—but ancient isn't the right word. "Ancient" is all that Greek and Roman junk they teach us about in school. "Ancient" is something people still kinda/sorta remember . . . still write books about. But these cities were SO MUCH OLDER than that. So old that anything else I could think of . . . the pyramids, the dinosaurs, even Gramma Esther . . . seemed BRAND NEW by comparison.

"What . . . what IS this place?" I asked.

The Warlock looked over at me and smiled. (I could tell that it really WAS a smile now. And a good one, too.) "These are the ruins . . . the echoes, if you will . . . of The Inconceivables That Have Been."

"Wait a minute—are you saying that the place up there . . . where Ija lives . . . isn't the ONLY Inconceivable?"

"The Inconceivable you know," the Warlock answered, "is only one of many that have occupied this place. Down here are ghosts that those who dwell above us—even Ija herself—cannot see. But I have asked the Purple Globe to open your eyes and widen your hearts—allowing you to glimpse not just the remnants of Inconceivables Long Gone—" Mother Pfoughh swam deeper . . . sailing straight for those ghost-cities . . . and they seemed to just dissolve into nothingness—or maybe vanish back into the past—as we glided through them. "—but the seeds of Inconceivables Yet To Be."

The Purple Globe beamed a wave of light out in front of us then, and dozens of OTHER bubble-cities shimmered into view. But these were different from the Inconceivables That Were. For one thing, they weren't ruins. In fact, they didn't really seem like cities at all . . . not in the way we understand them. They weren't built out of concrete and brick and glass. They were more like . . . living things. Almost like underwater plants . . . pushing up through the waves. And here's the part that's hardest to explain: it felt like those plant-cities weren't SURE yet what their true shapes were going to be. Like they were pushing this way . . . twisting that . . . trying—with all their hearts—to become something so completely new that it's NEVER EXISTED BEFORE IN ALL THE HISTORY OF ALL THE WORLDS THAT EVER WERE. (Hey, I told you this went way beyond words. Didn't believe me, did you?)

I looked over at the Warlock, and he had this sweet expression on his face—like he was a father. . . seeing his newborn baby for the first time. (And I had to wonder if Herbert the Great ever looked at ME that way.)

"Beautiful," he said, "isn't it, Kate?"

"Sure is," I answered . . . and I meant it, too. "Thanks, Uncle Waterlogged." (Hey, it just came out. I figured if Mother Pfoughh could call, him Uncle . . . why couldn't I? Besides, I never really HAD an uncle. My dad's an only child . . . and even though my mom's two sisters are married, I wouldn't call their loser-husbands Uncle if they PAID me.)

More Wubbtales—from little babies to some that were even bigger than Pfoughh—joined us then, gliding alongside and behind us. There must have been dozens of them. Hundreds, maybe. Uncle Waterlogged looked at that endless parade and then back over at me. "Thanks for what?" he asked.

"For showing me all this amazing stuff. I mean, where I come from we don't get to just look into the past . . . unless it's like an *I Love Lucy* rerun or something . . . and the closest I've ever come to seeing the future is in the fortune cookies at Hunan Kitchen."

He had no clue what I was babbling about . . . but he smiled anyway. "Time," the Warlock said, "has little meaning here. Past and future are far more fluid than most in your world ever dare imagine."

Now I had no clue what HE was talking about. "One thing I just don't get," I said, "is how there can BE other Inconceivables . . ."

Before he answered, the Warlock just sat there, all quiet—almost sad—and I had this weird feeling that he was . . . I dunno . . . translating something from a language that only he spoke. And he knew that, no matter how hard he tried . . . we'd never really understand.

"Abadazad," he finally said, "is in a

constant process of . . . well, some would call it perfecting—but that's a word I loathe. After all, how does one improve something that's ALREADY perfect?" He shook his head, and I could see he was struggling to find the right words. "But," he went on, "when a civilization exists, as ours does, without beginning or end—it's important that . . . from time to time . . . we RE-CREATE ourselves and start anew. Not because things are bad, mind you . . . but because they can always be BETTER."

He sat down on Mother Pfoughh's back then . . . and let out a fantastic sigh. He seemed suddenly exhausted . . . and more ancient than the oldest of the Old Cities. "So it is my role—assigned to me by the Floating Warlock himself—to sleep . . . and DREAM." He tilted his staff toward me, and I could feel the warm light of the globe on my face. "In concert with the Purple Globe, I sift through The Was . . . envision the Can Be . . . and let those dreams waft—like shimmering bubbles— across Abadazad . . ."

Okay, so I REALLY didn't understand most of what he said—but the thing is . . . it still felt true. You ever have that happen? You don't really GET something . . . but it feels true anyway? I was just about to explain that to Uncle Waterlogged, when Wix (the only person I've ever met with a mouth bigger than mine) butted in.

"Yeah, yeah," he said, waving his hand in disgust. "This is all fascinatin'! Now, if you're done talkin' in circles . . . can we get OUTTA here? In case y'didn't know, Kate's gotta save her brother!"

I would've been annoyed at the kid for interrupting, only I was even more annoyed at MYSELF—because Wix was right. (Again!) What was I doing swimming around down there? We had to get to the Wretchedly Awful City! We had to rescue Matty!

Uncle Waterlogged saw the panic in my eyes. "I DO know," he said. "That is precisely why I awakened . . . and returned here to Inconceivable."

"Whaddayou mean?" I asked.

The Warlock put out his hand, and there was a bubble there . . . the size of a basketball . . . balancing on his palm. And inside the bubble was the creepiest, ugliest, meanest face I've ever seen. A face I'd stared at one too many times in the pages of my Enchanted Diary: the Lanky Man.

"I felt you, Kate," Uncle Waterlogged said, "stirring the waters of my dreams."

"Me?"

"Oh, yes. I've known of your coming for some time." I couldn't stand looking at that Lanky Creep, so I jabbed the bubble with my finger and popped it . . . popping Lanks along with it. But then another bubble wafted down onto the Warlock's palm . . . and this time MY BROTHER'S FACE was glimmering inside.

Matty looked the way he did when the Enchanted Diary showed me Lanky Man's laboratory. The poor kid seemed asleep . . . but NOT asleep. Like he was in some kind of weird trance or something. All I wanted to do was reach in there and hold my brother. Promise him that everything was going to be all right. ~~That I wouldn't let him down again.~~

But when I grabbed for the bubble, it bobbed up out of Uncle Waterlogged's hand—joining a couple dozen MORE bubbles that suddenly appeared . . . floating on the water all around us. There were kids in each one—some of them couldn't have been more than two or three years old—zombied-out, just like Matt.

"Kate," Uncle Waterlogged said, and he seemed angry again, not at Wix or me but at the Lanky Man and all he'd done, "you're the ONLY ONE who can stop the Lanky Man . . . and free not just your brother . . . but ALL the human children he's kidnapped."

Hearing that kind of made my stomach turn inside out. "But," I stuttered, "but it's gonna be hard enough just getting Matt out! How can—?"

The Warlock gave me this look . . . like he felt sorry for me or something. "I simply dream these things, Kate," he sighed. "YOU have to live them."

Which seemed like the dumbest answer I'd ever heard. "Now . . . now WAIT a minute!" I yelled, stomping back and forth on Pfoughh's back. "You've got all these people running around with magic dripping out of their noses . . . and you expect some immature jerk who flunked algebra twice . . . TWICE . . . t'save the day? Why can't Queen Ija do it? Why can't you?"

"Because," the Warlock answered calmly, "it isn't OUR destiny. It's YOURS."

"I don't understand ANY of this!" I screamed . . . and then Idiot Me stomps right off Mother Pfoughh's back and drops—WAY too fast—toward the bottomless bottom of the canal.

Pfoughh sort of rolled her bulk over a little and scooped me up, very gently, into the nook of her tusks. "Perhaps," she said, her foghorn voice vibrating through my whole body, "you . . . don't . . . have . . . to. The . . . mind . . . is . . . a . . . limited . . . instrument.

Why . . . don't . . . you . . . LISTEN . . . Kate?
Listen . . . with . . . your . . . HEART?"

The other Wubbtales came gliding toward
us then . . . swimming in circles around Mother
Pfoughh. I was curled up in Pfoughh's tusks,
watching them pirouette around us like dancers
in some kind of underwater ballet.

And they SANG to me. ALL THE WUBBTALES
SANG.

Sang like . . . how can I ever explain it?

Like the way I remember Frantic Frances
singing to Matt right after he was born.

It's not that my mother had such a great
voice—I mean, the woman could barely carry
a tune—but she was so happy then . . . so
crazy about the squirt that—for a little
while, at least—she forgot about her
biweekly nervous breakdowns. And when
she'd sing him some dumb little song—y'know,
"Hush Little Baby, Don't You Cry," that kind
of junk—you could HEAR the way she loved
Matty. Hear it better than when she said it
in words.

But the thing about the Wubbtales is that
they didn't sing like ONE mother . . . they sang
like every mother in the history of . . .

the countless centuries of Ija's reign.

Despite this, her reaction was quite understandable; for these three astounding beings were none other than the legendary Elders of Abadazad. There they stood: the Sprouting Sorceress, with her bountiful hair of vines, flowers, and leaves, and lips the color of fresh blueberries; the Landlocked Warlock, with his mountainous head of chiseled granite and hands of finest marble; and the Burning Witch, draped in an exquisite gown composed of living flames, its beauty not only matched but surpassed by the gorgeous creature wearing it.

The Queen had met them all before, of course, but only rarely, and never gathered in her father's company like this. In fact, it was written in the Book of Koob that the four Elders—the fourth being Ija's beloved Uncle Waterlogged, who, at that moment, was sleeping, serenely oblivious, in the gardens below—had not even seen each other since the day the Floating Warlock first breathed Abadazad into Being. (Royal Historians would say this is an exaggeration, but if so, only slightly.)

"You appear," intoned the King, with amused under-

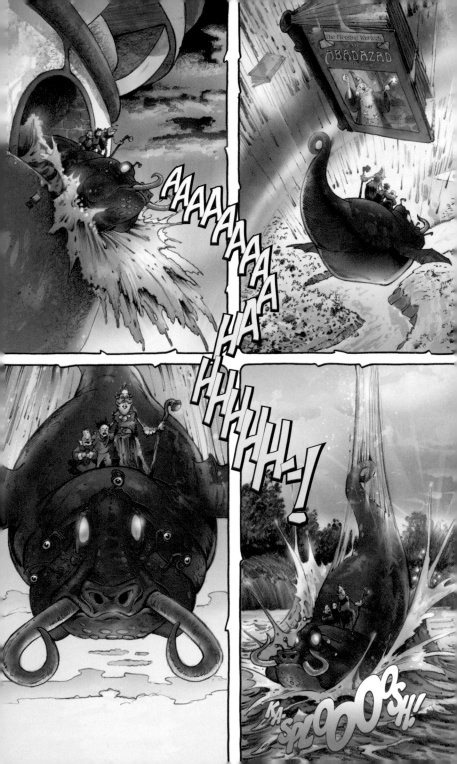

I held on to Uncle Waterlogged's hand for dear life . . . Wix held on to mine . . . and Mother Pfoughh tore straight up that river . . . leaving Inconceivable far behind us. I thought about Queen Ija up there . . . Little Martha . . . all those people waiting for me at the party— and, yeah, I felt a little sad. But I felt excited, too. More than that, I felt hope.

"What now, Uncle Waterlogged?" I asked.

"We'll travel east together on the Evermore River," he said, "then you'll turn north toward the Edges of Abadazad . . . while I move southward into the Ocean of Light." He pointed his staff into the distance . . . toward some faraway goal that only he could see. "I've been away from the sea too long."

Pfoughh picked up speed . . . Wixy and I plopped down and got comfortable (well, as comfortable as you can get on the back of a giant whale-thing). "How long?" I asked the Warlock.

"Perhaps one or two of your hours, Kate. Is that all right?"

Uncle Waterlogged had a lousy sense of time—most Abadazadians do—because one or two hours turned out to be more like seven or eight. But I didn't mind. We didn't say much . . . but every once in a while Wix would make some stupid joke (and, okay, I laughed at most of them) or the Warlock would point out something interesting, like a school of Boomeranguppies swimming by or a herd of wild Trunkmonkeys swinging through the trees. We stopped once to eat, too, porking out in a riverside grove of Dinner Trees (I made sure to stuff my backpack full of food) . . . but mostly we were just quiet. Not UNCOMFORTABLE quiet. GOOD quiet.

I felt . . . well, kinda the way it used to be on those really hot Brooklyn days when my parents would take us down to Manhattan Beach. Mom hated the beach, so she'd slop two hundred layers of suntan lotion on herself and sit on the blanket, under an umbrella, reading.

My brother was little then—all those big waves kinda scared him—so Herbert would just lie there with us right where the surf met the shore: Matty in one arm, me in the other. The water'd roll in around us, then roll out again . . . and it was like there was nothing in the whole world that could ever hurt us. Like, no matter what went wrong, Dad would always be there to protect us.

But as soon as I felt Mother Pfoughh slow down, angling in toward a little cove, I felt like a complete idiot for even THINKING about that stuff.

"This," the Warlock said, "is where we part, Kate."

Wix got this idiot grin on his face, shouted "At last!" and swan-dived off the Wubbtale's back, splashing straight toward dry land.

Me? I turned on the Patented Jameson Glare. Times TEN.

Look, I know Uncle Waterlogged told me he was heading out to the Ocean of Light . . . but I guess, deep down, I didn't believe him. I mean, this wasn't some jerk like my father . . . he was Queen Ija's uncle. He was the Waterlogged Warlock, for crying out loud. And guys like that didn't just up and ditch kids.

I TOLD him so, too.

"I'm not ditching you," he said.

"Yes, you are!" I huffed, turning my back on him—not just 'cause I was mad, but because I felt like I was gonna cry (guess Queen Ija's Weeping Spell hadn't completely worn off). "So go on! Leave! See if I care!"

Uncle Waterlogged eased over to me, his

webbed feet slapping gently against Pfoughh's back. "Kate, Kate," he said—and he sounded like HE was gonna cry, too, "I'm truly sorry—but I have no choice."

I whirled around then . . . so mad I could have punched him. "No choice?" I shouted. "That's the stupidest thing I've ever heard in my life! EVERYBODY'S got a choice!"

He reached out to take my hand—and I backed away. "Do you remember," he sighed, "in Mr. Davies's books . . . how the Waterlogged Warlock must return to the deeps of the deepest oceans—or he'll die of a broken heart?" And I could tell by the way he said it that Franklin O. Davies didn't make THAT one up. It was true. And I didn't want Uncle Waterlogged to die.

But I didn't want him to go, either.

"Please," I said—and the waterworks were REALLY flowing now. "PLEASE don't go. There's gotta be SOME way you can stay. Some magic that—"

He dropped down to one knee and stretched out his arms to me. "You have to understand, Kate," he said, smiling (and it was maybe the saddest smile I'd ever seen),

"I'm not IN the NEXT CHAPTER."

Soon as he said that I knew what he meant. It was all that annoying stuff about destiny again. How I was the one who had to do this, not him. How no matter how much he WANTED to come with me—and I know he did . . . with all his heart!—he just couldn't.

And all of a sudden I felt worse for him than I did for me. I threw myself into the Warlock's arms and held on to him so tight I thought my ribs were gonna crack. But even if they did, I would've KEPT holding on. Because he WAS my uncle, wasn't he? And he was my friend. (Funny how a kid like me . . . who didn't have many friends—or even one—was suddenly finding them everywhere she looked.)

"Oh, Uncle Waterlogged," I said. "What are we gonna do? Wix . . . he's just a kid. If we're all alone out there, then the Lanky Man might—"

"Do you remember what Great Auntie Nott told you about magic?"

I thought about it for a second, and then I nodded. "Y'mean about it being something really PERSONAL?"

"Exactly," Uncle Waterlogged said. "And this—" He reached out and touched the pearl necklace he'd given me. "This is YOUR personal magic. It will help you, Kate . . . in ways you can't yet imagine."

I held tight to the pearl for a couple of seconds then looked up at Uncle Waterlogged. "Hey," I said, suddenly realizing, "how'd YOU know what Auntie Nott told me?"

"Trade secret," he said, twirling his staff and sending out a wave of purple light that wrapped itself around me like a purple snake . . . whipping me into the air and carrying me above the shallows and safely onto shore.

Wix was waiting for me, tugging on my arm, hopping up and down like a frog and telling me to "Come on, come ON, let's go!"

I turned back to say good-bye to Uncle Waterlogged, but Mother Pfoughh had already sailed out of the cove. She was singing again—a song as deep and blue as the Eight Oceans. The Waterlogged Warlock looked back—like he knew I was watching—but only for a second. Then he turned around . . . just as the giant Wubbtale shot high into the air . . . then dove beneath the surface of the river—

And vanished.

I probably would have stood there all day waiting to see if they'd come back up again, but

Little Mr. Ants-in-His-Pants was already halfway up the hill, heading for the woods. "Come on, come on, come ON!" he said again.

"'Bye, Uncle Waterlogged," I sighed—then I climbed the hill after Wixy.

So here I am—the girl who dropped out of Brownies after three weeks—sitting in a little clearing on the edge of the Nevermore Forest (I'm glad the Warlock gave me my clothes back . . . 'cause it sure is chilly here), . . . writing in my diary by the light of a campfire that Master Wix lit with his HEAD. Guess there are advantages to hanging with living candles, huh?

I'd be lying if I said I wasn't a little worried (maybe even slightly panic-stricken). I mean, we're here in the Middle of Absolute Nowhere . . . we've only got enough food for two or three days . . . and, really, I have NO CLUE how to get to the Wretchedly Awful City. (Wix says he does, but between you and me, I'm not sure I believe him.)

Then I look down at the pearl around my neck. At that incredible picture of me and my brother . . . together again in a Future That Might Be. That HAS to be.

My Own Personal Magic, Uncle Waterlogged called it.

I'll be there soon, Matty.

I PROMISE.

. . . to be continued

You think all THAT was
weirdoramic—wait'll you see
the stuff that's coming UP. . . .

I'd tell you who THIS guy is . . . but you'd never believe me. Let's just say that Franklin O. Davies got it wrong. AGAIN.

Don't let the cute face fool you. Get too close . . . and you're Dragon Buffet.

I've had to deal with my share of
two-faced girls at school . . . but
not like THIS.

Geppetto wouldn't want anything
to do with THIS puppet.

Here are the books in the
ABADAZAD series—so far . . .

ABADAZAD No. 1
The Road to Inconceivable

ABADAZAD No. 2
The Dream Thief

And coming soon . . .

ABADAZAD No. 3
The Puppet, the Professor,
and the Prophet

ABADAZAD

THE DREAM THIEF

by J.M. DeMatteis

drawings by Mike Ploog

colors by Nick Bell

HYPERION BOOKS FOR CHILDREN
NEW YORK

Text by J.M. DeMatteis
Art by Mike Ploog

Printed in the United States of America

First Edition

10 9 8 7 6 5 4 3 2 1

This book is set in CF Whisper.

Reinforced binding

ISBN 1-4231-0064-6

Library of Congress Cataloging-in-Publication Data on file.

Visit www.hyperionbooksforchildren.com

Managing Editors: Jaime Herbeck, Janet Castiglione
Copy Chief: Monica Mayper
Book Designer: Roberta Pressel
Production Artist: Debbie Lofaso
Production Manager: Nisha Panchal

For my mother, Bea—who, I suspect,
is sharing a box of jelly candies with
Queen Ija and the Floating Warlock . . .
somewhere in Abadazad.

—JMD

In memory of my dad,
Raymond Joseph "Red" Ploog,
1910–1978.

—MP